# What's for Dinner, Mom?

Victoria Tydings Strand

To order additional copies of this book, contact:
Xlibris
1-888-795-4274
www.Xlibris.com
Orders@Xlibris.com

This book is dedicated to Johnny,
Lisa, Elizabeth, Ingrid, Alexandra,
Hadley, Maisy, and Ed!

# What's for Dinner, Mom?

One Saturday as the girls ran through the lush, green lawn in front of their house, Alex asked Hadley, "What should we do today?

'" Do you want to play dress-ups?' Hadley asked, 'No,' replied Alex, 'I played dress-ups at school yesterday." Alex looked up and noticed the soccer ball by the step. "What about kicking the ball around the yard, asked Alex?" Hadley said, "No, I am tired from soccer practice this morning."

The girls sat across from each other and Hadley started to smile as she stood up. "I know!" said Hadley, "Let's pretend to be Mom and make up silly and crazy dinners for each other!" "Wow," said Alex, "that sounds scrumptious!" "Can I be first?" asked Alex. "Ok," answered Hadley.

Hadley said to Alex, "I'll make my food at the bottom of the steps." Alex said, "I'll work on the right side of the porch." "Sounds good," answered, Hadley. As the girls ran off to get their supplies, Alex said, "Let's start in 10 minutes."

The girls ran into the house giggling. Hadley said, "My food is going to be funny." As Alex went up the stairs to get supplies, she yelled, "My food is going to be weird!"

After both girls gathered what they needed, they started putting their creations together. A few minutes later, Alex yelled to Hadley to come up on the porch. Alex said that she was thrilled about the new game.

Hadley walked over to Alex's spot and asked in a crazy voice, "What's for dinner, Mom?" "I have some delicious creamed tennis shoes, dear!" Hadley pretend to taste the creamy, rubbery mess. "This is so smooth and white," stated Hadley. "Ok, "said, Hadley "now, please come and see what I made."

Alex ran after Hadley. With excitement, Alex asked, "What's for dinner, Mom?" Hadley replied, "How does a bowl of soft, sock stew sound, darling?" Alex took a pretend sip and commented, "The soft socks are so stretchy and stinky!"

The girls went back and forth laughing. Next, Alex asked Hadley, "How do grass sandwiches sound, precious?" Hadley said, "They look green and chewy!"

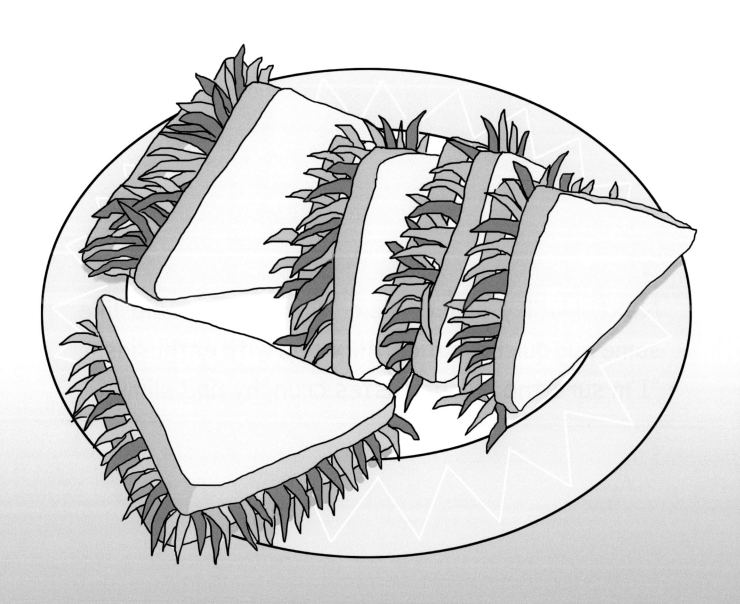

Next, Hadley asked Alex, "I bet you would like some bug quiche, cutie!" Alex said with enthusiasm, "I'm sure the quiche tastes crunchy and slimy!"

Alex said, "Hadley, the leaf and twig soup looks very tasty, my little one. Please eat every bite."

"Would you like chips with your chunky, mud burger sweetie? Hadley asked Alex.

23

Alex then asked Hadley, "Look, how colorful the crayon melt turned out, honey?"

Hadley showed Alex the dainty flower petal salad. "Cupcake, Hadley said, I bet those petals will taste velvety!

Hadley tilted her head and announced, "I'm ready for dessert." Alex said, "My lumpy, pebble pudding will be good for your teeth, darling!" Hadley was amused as she told Alex about the milky white paste and glue popsicles!" Alex made a face.

"Are you tired of playing the, "What's for dinner, Mom?" game?" Hadley asked Alex. "Yes" said Alex. Both exhausted girls looked at the mess and knew they needed to clean it up.

But, just around the corner their Mom, with a big smile, appeared. Would you two like hamburgers, fruit and ice cream for dinner? Both girls shook their heads in agreement and said, "Yes, that dinner sounds yummy and normal!" Thanks, Mom!

Printed in the United States
By Bookmasters